Cub's First Summer

by Rebecca Elliott

Licensed exclusively to Top That Publishing Ltd
Tide Mill Way, Woodbridge, Suffolk, IP12 1AP, UK
www.topthatpublishing.com
Copyright © 2012 Rebecca Elliott
All rights reserved
2 4 6 8 9 7 5 3 1
Manufactured in China

Written and illustrated by Rebecca Elliott

ISBN 978-1-78244-016-1

A catalogue record for this book is available from the British Library

'For my little cubs – Clemmie and Toby. x'

It was the first day of summer and Cub had just woken up.
'Good morning,' said Mum. 'Let's go and explore the forest.
Come on ...'

'Why is it so hot?'
asked Cub.

'So that we can splash in the cool water!' giggled Mum.

And the sun shone down.

'Why are the crickets so loud?' asked Cub.

'Because they want us to jump high like them!' exclaimed Mum.

And the sun grew hazy.

'Why are the days so long?' asked Cub.

And clouds began
to gather in the sky.

'Why are the birds singing so loudly?' asked Cub.

'So that we can dance to their music!' sang Mum.

And the clouds got darker.

'Why are the bees so busy?' asked Cub.
'Because they want to make us lots of
yummy honey!' said Mum.

And the air
grew heavy.

'Why are the vegetables so big?' asked Cub.

'So that we can feast on them!' spluttered Mum,
with her mouth full of carrot.
And the first flash of lightning lit up the sky.

'What's that noise?' asked Cub, as the first rumble of thunder grumbled all around him.

'Oh no!' gasped Mum.
'Quick! Follow me before the thunderstorm gets worse!'

And back they went through the vegetable patch, past the trees, back and forth through the meadow, and over the river until, at last, they found their way home!

'Why is the thunderstorm
so scary?' asked Cub.

'So that we can
snuggle up tight,'
whispered Mum,
with a smile.

'Why am I so tired?' yawned Cub.
'Because it is sleepy time,' murmured Mum.
'Night night, little cub.'